The Jungle Book

*Retold from the Rudyard Kipling original
by Lisa Church*

Illustrated by Lucy Corvino

STERLING CHILDREN'S BOOKS
New York

STERLING CHILDREN'S BOOKS
New York

An Imprint of Sterling Publishing
387 Park Avenue South
New York, NY 10016

ISBN 978-1-4027-4576-8

Library of Congress Cataloging-in-Publication Data

Church, Lisa R., 1960–
 The jungle book / retold from the Rudyard Kipling original ; abridged by
Lisa Church ; illustrated by Lucy Corvino ; afterword by Arthur Pober.
   p. cm.—(Classic starts)
 Summary: An abridged retelling of the adventures of Mowgli, a boy reared by a pack of wolves,
and the wild animals of the jungle.
 ISBN 978-1-4027-4576-8
 [1. Jungles—Fiction. 2. Animals—Fiction. 3. India—Fiction.] I. Corvino, Lucy, ill. II. Kipling,
Rudyard, 1865–1936. Jungle book. III. Title.

PZ7.C4703Ju 2007
[Fic]—dc22

2007003948

Distributed in Canada by Sterling Publishing
c/o Canadian Manda Group, 165 Dufferin Street,
Toronto, Ontario, Canada M6K 3H6
Distributed in the United Kingdom by GMC Distribution Services,
Castle Place, 166 High Street, Lewes, East Sussex, England BN7 1XU
Distributed in Australia by Capricorn Link (Australia) Pty. Ltd.
P.O. Box 704, Windsor, NSW 2756, Australia

For information about custom editions, special sales, and premium and corporate purchases,
please contact Sterling Special Sales at 800-805-5489 or specialsales@sterlingpublishing.com.

Printed in China
Lot#:
4 6 8 10 9 7 5
11/12

www.sterlingpublishing.com/kids

CONTENTS

CHAPTER 1

Mowgli's Brothers

ᘓ

It was seven o'clock on a very warm evening in the Seeonee hills when Father Wolf woke up from his day's rest. He scratched, yawned, and looked at Mother Wolf with her big gray nose dropped across her four squealing cubs.

"Augrh!" said Father Wolf. "It's time to hunt again."

He was on his way out of the cave when he saw the jackal—Tabaqui—approaching. The jungle wolves of India hated Tabaqui because he ran about making trouble, telling lies, and eating garbage from the nearby village. However, he did always know the happenings of the jungle.

Tabaqui told Father Wolf that he had some troubling news.

"Shere Khan, the Big One, has moved his hunting grounds," Tabaqui said. "He will hunt here for the next moon."

Shere Khan was the tiger who lived near the Waingunga River, twenty miles away.

"He can't do that!" Father Wolf said angrily. "He will scare away the animals I hunt!"

"Why is everyone so afraid of Shere Khan?" said Mother Wolf. "He has limped on one foot since he was born and cannot hurt the jungle animals. That's why he kills the village cattle. But now the people of the village will hunt him. We will need to run when they start the chase."

Father Wolf listened carefully and heard the dry, angry whine of a tiger who has caught nothing and does not care if all the jungle knows it.

"Listen to that howl! It is the sound he makes when he hunts Man," Mother Wolf said softly.

"Man!" said Father Wolf. "Are there so few beetles and frogs that he must eat Man?"

Father Wolf knew that the Law of the Jungle did not allow any beast to eat Man unless he was killing to show his children how to kill.

"Sooner or later, Man will be back with guns," Mother Wolf said. "Everyone in the jungle will suffer."

"Something is coming uphill!" said Father Wolf, twitching one ear. "Get ready!"

The bushes moved in the thicket, and Father Wolf dropped down to see what came out. He pounced—and then, if you had been watching, you would have seen the most wonderful thing in the world. The wolf stopped in midair. He came back down, landing right where he started.

"Man!" he snapped. "A man cub. Look!"

Right in front of him, holding on to a low

branch, stood a little baby, soft and slightly chubby, who could just walk. He looked up at Father Wolf's face and laughed.

"That's a man cub?" said Mother Wolf. "I've never seen one. Bring it here. How little! How brave!" she added softly.

In the next second, the moonlight was blocked out of the cave. The square head of the tiger Shere Khan appeared in the doorway, his body too big to fit through the small opening.

"A man cub went this way," said the tiger. "Its parents have run off. Give the cub to me."

Father Wolf knew the man cub would be in danger if he was handed over to Shere Khan.

"The wolves are free animals," said Father Wolf. "They take orders from the head of the Wolf Pack, not from a striped cattle killer like you! The man cub is ours to do with as we choose."

"This is I, Shere Khan, who speaks to you!" the tiger roared, filling the cave with thunder.

"And it is I, Raksha, who answers," said Mother Wolf angrily. "The man cub is mine! He shall not be killed! He will run with my Pack and hunt with my Pack. In the end, you hunter of man cubs, you frog eater and fish killer . . . he will hunt *you!* Now go!"

Shere Khan knew better than to fight Mother Wolf. Even he could not best a mother fighting for the life of her child. He backed up, growling, his head twisting to get out of the cave. When he was outside, he shouted, "You may say this now, but we shall see what the whole Pack says. That cub is mine, and to my teeth he will come in the end!"

Mother Wolf threw herself down among her cubs. "Shere Khan is right," Father Wolf said to her softly. "The cub must be shown to the Pack. Will you still keep him?"

"Keep him?" she gasped. "He came hungry and alone in the night, and yet he wasn't afraid. Of course I will keep him. Lie still, Mowgli the Frog. This is the name I will call you."

"But what will our Pack say?" said Father Wolf. "The Law of the Jungle says that cubs must be brought to the Pack as soon as they are old enough."

"We shall see," said Mother Wolf. "We shall see."

Time passed, and the man cub stayed with Mother and Father Wolf. They waited until their cubs could run a little, and then took the young wolves and Mowgli to the Council Rock. The rock was a hilltop covered with stones and boulders where a hundred wolves could hide. Akela, the great gray Lone Wolf who led all the Pack by strength and intelligence, led the meeting.

There was very little talking at the Rock. The cubs tumbled over one another in the center of the circle, where their mothers and fathers sat. Sometimes a mother would push her cub far out into the moonlight to be sure it was seen.

At last, Father Wolf pushed Mowgli the Frog into the center. Akela never raised his head from his paws. A muffled voice from behind the rocks called out, "The cub is mine. Give him to me!"

Shere Khan's cry did not work. Instead, there was a chorus of deep growls. Then a young wolf spoke out, questioning why the man cub was there.

Now, the Law of the Jungle says that if there is any question about a cub being accepted by the Pack, two members of the Pack must speak on why he should be taken in. These two members cannot be the cub's mother or father.

"Who speaks for the man cub?" asked Akela. There was no answer, and Mother Wolf got ready for what she knew would be a fight.

Then Baloo — the only other creature that was allowed at the Pack Council — got up on his hind legs and grunted. The sleepy brown bear taught the Law of the Jungle to all wolf cubs, and was respected among the senior wolves.

"I speak for the man cub," he said. "There is nothing wrong with having a man cub in our Pack. I myself will teach him."

"We need another," said Akela. "Baloo has

spoken, and he is the teacher of our young cubs. Who speaks besides Baloo?"

A black shadow dropped down into the circle. It was Bagheera, the black panther. Everyone knew him, but nobody cared to cross his path. He was as sneaky as Tabaqui, as bold as a wild buffalo, and as reckless as a hurt elephant. But he had a voice as soft as wild honey dripping from a tree, and skin softer than the down of a baby bird.

"Baloo has spoken for him; now I will speak, too. Will you take a bull, fat and freshly killed, in exchange for accepting this man cub?" Bagheera asked.

The members of the Pack looked at one another. The panther should not even be at the meeting, but offering such a prize was tempting. The Pack agreed. Then, one by one, they slowly left to see the freshly killed bull. Shere Khan roared in the night, for he was angry that Mowgli had not been handed over.

"Roar well," said Bagheera, "for someday this man cub's roar will be of importance."

"Take the man cub away," Akela said to Father Wolf, "and train him well. Men and their cubs are very wise. He may be of help someday."

But only time would tell if this would be true.

⌒

Now, you will just have to be happy with guessing at the wonderful life Mowgli had among the wolves for the next ten or eleven years. If it were all to be written down, it would fill so many books!

He grew up with the cubs, even though they were grown wolves almost before he was a child. Father Wolf taught him everything he needed to know about the jungle. Every rustle in the grass, every breath of the warm night air, every note of the owls above his head, every scratch of a bat's claws, and every splash of every little fish jumping in a pool meant just as much to Father Wolf as the work of an office means to a businessman. When he was not learning, Mowgli sat out in the sun and slept, and ate, and slept again. When he felt dirty or hot, he swam in the forest pools. When he wanted honey, he climbed a tree for it. At first Mowgli clung to the branches. But as he learned, he flung himself through the branches, almost as boldly as the gray apes of the jungle.

More than anything, Mowgli loved to walk into the dark warm heart of the forest with Bagheera, sleep all through the drowsy day, and watch Bagheera do his killing at night. Bagheera killed right and left when he felt hungry. When the man cub was old enough to understand things, Bagheera explained that he must never touch cattle because he had been bought into the

Pack for the price of a bull's life. Aside from cattle, the jungle offered him all the food he would ever need.

Under the jungle animals' watch, the man cub grew and grew strong. He didn't know that he was learning many lessons while he was hunting for food every day. He found which plants were safe to eat, which animals he was able to catch, and how many bugs made a crunchy and filling supper.

Mother Wolf told Mowgli once or twice that Shere Khan was not to be trusted, and that some-day he must kill the tiger. A young wolf would have remembered that every hour, but Mowgli forgot it because he was only a young boy.

Shere Khan often crossed his path in the jungle, for as Akela grew older and weaker, the limping tiger came to be friends with the younger wolves of the Pack. They followed him along, looking for scraps. Shere Khan was amazed that the Pack was still willing to follow a dying wolf and a man cub. He teased them sometimes, arguing that he would make a much better leader than what they had now.

Bagheera knew of Shere Khan's thoughts, and told Mowgli that the limping tiger would kill him someday if he wasn't careful. But Mowgli only laughed and answered, "I have the Pack and you and Baloo. Why should I be afraid?"

"Little Brother, open those eyes. Shere Khan did not kill you in the jungle, but remember, Akela is very old. Soon the day will come when he is leader no more. Many of the wolves believe that a man cub has no place with the Pack. In a little time, you will be a man."

"And why shouldn't a man run with his brothers?" asked Mowgli. "I was born in the jungle. I have obeyed the Law of the Jungle, and there is no wolf I have not helped. Surely they are my brothers!"

Bagheera stretched and half shut his eyes. "Little Brother," he said, "feel under my jaw."

Mowgli put his strong hand just under Bagheera's silky chin. He came upon a little bald spot.

"There is no one in the jungle who knows I carry that mark—the mark of a collar. And yet, Little Brother, I was born among men. It was in the care of these men that my mother died—in the cages of the King's Palace. It was because of this that I paid the price for you at the Council Meeting when you were a tiny man cub. I did not want you to be raised by men. Yes, I, too, was born among men. They kept me behind bars and fed me from an iron pan, until one night I got so angry I broke the silly lock with one blow of my paw and ran away. I became more terrible in the jungle than even Shere Khan."

"Yes," said Mowgli. "All the jungle fears Bagheera—all except me."

"Oh, you are a man cub," said the black panther very tenderly. "And as I returned to the jungle, so must you go back to men at last—to the men who are your brothers—if you are not killed at the Council."

"But why—why should anyone wish to kill me?" asked Mowgli.

"Look at me," said Bagheera, and Mowgli looked at him between the eyes. The big panther turned his head away.

"*That* is why," he said, moving his paw in the leaves. "Not even I can look you between the eyes, and I was born among men, and I love you, Little Brother. The others hate you because their eyes cannot meet yours—because you have shown us since you were a young child that you are wise— because you have pulled out thorns from their feet—because you are a man."

"I did not know these things," said Mowgli sadly, and he frowned under his heavy black eyebrows.

"You must be ready for the Council at the

Rock when the Pack turns against Akela. You will need to . . . to . . . I have it!" said Bagheera, leaping up. "Go down quickly to the men's huts in the valley. Take some of the Red Flower they grow there. The Red Flower is a stronger friend than I or Baloo or anyone in the Pack who loves you. You must have it ready."

By Red Flower, Bagheera meant fire, but no creature in the jungle called it that name. Every beast lived in great fear of it, because they didn't understand it.

"The Red Flower?" said Mowgli. "That grows outside their huts in the night? Yes, I will get some."

"Now that is how a wise man cub speaks!" Bagheera said proudly. "Remember that it grows in little pots. Get one quickly, and keep it by you for when you need it."

"Good!" said Mowgli. "I go. But are you sure that Shere Khan is worth all this trouble?"

"I am sure, Little Brother."

"Then I shall pay him back for all that he has done . . . and maybe a little more," Mowgli said as he skipped away.

Mowgli followed the cries of the hunting Pack to the stream. The snort of a buck caused his ears to prick, and he listened to the howls from the young wolves. "Akela! Akela! Attack now, Akela! You are the Lone Wolf! Show your strength!" They expected their leader to miss his prey. His age made him slow and cautious.

The Lone Wolf must have sprung and missed the deer, for Mowgli heard the snap of his teeth and then a yelp as the buck kicked him over.

Mowgli didn't wait to hear anything more. He dashed on and let the yells grow fainter behind him as he ran into the fields where the villagers lived.

Tomorrow is the day for Akela and me, Mowgli thought as he pressed his face close to the window of a hut. *He can no longer prove his leadership. Death is near for him. I must get the Red Flower.*

He watched the fire on the hearth all night and saw the woman of the house get up and feed it in the darkness. When morning came and most of the area around the Red Flower was cold and white, Mowgli watched a man child pick up a pot and fill it with lumps of red-hot charcoal. The child put it under his blanket and went outside to milk the cows.

Is that all? thought Mowgli. *If a cub can do it, there is nothing to fear.* He quietly walked around the corner, took the pot from the boy's hands, and disappeared into the fog while the boy cried out in fear.

They are very like me, Mowgli thought, blowing into the pot as he had seen the woman do. *This "thing" will die if I do not give it something to eat.* He dropped twigs and dried bark on the red stuff. Halfway back to the jungle, he met Bagheera.

"They are looking for you," said the panther.

"I am ready. See!" Mowgli held up the firepot.

Akela the Lone Wolf lay by the side of his rock as a sign that the leadership of the Pack was open.

Shere Khan walked back and forth in front of the Pack. Some hungry wolves tagged along behind him. Bagheera lay close to Mowgli. The firepot was between Mowgli's knees. When the Pack was all gathered together, Shere Khan began to speak.

"He has no right to speak," whispered Bagheera. "Tell them, Mowgli!"

Mowgli sprang to his feet. "Free animals," he cried, "does Shere Khan lead our Pack? What has a tiger to do with our leadership?"

"I see that you are looking for new leadership . . . and I have been asked to speak—" Shere Khan began.

"By whom?" asked Mowgli. "The leadership of the Pack should stay with the wolves!"

There were yells from the crowd for Mowgli to stay quiet. Akela raised his old head wearily.

"Forget this old wolf!" Shere Khan said, looking at Akela. "He is doomed to die! His years have passed. He has had his turn leading the Pack. It is the man cub who has lived too long. He has troubled the jungle for ten seasons now. Give him to me or I will hunt here always and not give you one bone. He is a man and I hate him!"

More than half the Pack yelled back. "A man! A man! Let him go to his own place!"

"And turn all the people of the village against us?" shouted Shere Khan. "No! Give him to me. He is a man, and none of us can look him between the eyes. He is dangerous."

Akela lifted his head again and said, "He has eaten our food. He has slept with us. He has hunted game with us. He has broken no Law of the Jungle."

"No man cub can run with the people of the jungle," howled Shere Khan. "Give him to me!"

"He is our brother in all but blood," Akela went on, "and you would kill him here? I will make you a promise. If you let the man cub go to his own place, I will not fight back when it is my turn to die."

"He is a man—a man—a man!" snarled the Pack.

"It is up to you now," Bagheera said to Mowgli. "We can do no more except fight."

Mowgli stood upright with the firepot in his hands. He stretched out his arms and spoke with rage and sorrow. "Listen you, who have told me so often tonight that I am a man that I feel your words are true. I will not call you brothers any longer. What you do, and what you will not do, is not yours to say. I will make those choices."

He flung his pot on the ground, and some of

the red coals lit a tuft of dried moss on fire. All the Council leaned back in fear before the leaping flames.

Mowgli pushed a dead branch into the fire until the twigs lit and crackled. He twirled it above his head among the frightened wolves.

"You are the Master," said Bagheera. "Save Akela from his death. He has always been your friend."

Mowgli looked over the Pack. "I will go back to my own people as you wish. I will forget your friendship. But I will be more loyal than you. I promise there will be no war between any of my people and the Pack. Yet there is one thing I must settle before I go."

He slowly walked forward to where Shere Khan sat blinking stupidly at the flames and lifted him up by the tuft of fur under his chin.

"Get up when a man speaks to you!" Mowgli cried.

Shere Khan's ears lay flat back on his head, and he shut his eyes, for the burning twig was very near.

"This beast said he would kill me at the Council. You move a whisker toward me and I will push this Red Flower down your throat!"

The tiger whimpered and whined in fear.

"Pah! You jungle cat! Go now! But remember this: The next time I come to the Council Rock, it will be with Shere Khan's hide. For the rest, Akela goes free to live as he pleases. You will not hurt him. You other dogs, leave!"

The fire at the end of the branch was burning brightly now, and the wolves scurried off as Mowgli ran the twig around the circle of the Pack. At last there were only Akela, Bagheera, and perhaps ten wolves who had taken Mowgli's side. Then something inside Mowgli began to hurt as he had never hurt before in his life. He caught his breath and sobbed. The tears ran down his face.

"What is it?" Bagheera asked.

"I do not wish to leave the jungle, and I don't know why I feel this way. Am I dying, Bagheera?"

"No, Little Brother. Those are only tears that men use," said Bagheera. "Now I know for certain that you are a man and a man cub no longer. The jungle is shut to you from now on. Let them fall, Mowgli. They are only tears." So Mowgli sat and cried as if his heart would break, for he had never really cried in all his life before.

"Now," he said, "I will go to men. But first I must say good-bye to my mother." And so he went to the cave where she lived with Father Wolf, and he cried on her fur while the four almost-grown cubs around her howled sadly.

"You will not forget me?" said Mowgli.

"Never," said the cubs. "Come to the foot of the hill when you are a man and we will talk to you. We will go to the cornfields to play with you at night."

"Come soon!" said Father Wolf. "Oh, wise little frog, come again soon. Your mother and I are growing old."

"Come soon, little son of mine," said Mother Wolf. "For listen, child of Man, I love you more than I have ever loved my cubs."

"I will surely come," said Mowgli. "Don't forget me! Tell them in the jungle never to forget me!"

The dawn had begun to break when Mowgli went down the hillside alone. It was time to meet those strange things called men.

CHAPTER 2

Kaa's Hunting

~

All that is told here happened some time before Mowgli left the Seeonee Wolf Pack and promised to get back at Shere Khan the tiger. It was in the days when Baloo was teaching Mowgli the Law of the Jungle. The big, serious old brown bear was happy to have such a fine student. The young wolves he usually taught only listened long enough to learn the Hunting Verse: *Feet that make no noise, eyes that can see in the dark, ears that can hear in the blowing wind, and sharp white teeth—all these things are signs of our brothers. Except—Tabaqui the jackal, and the hyena whom we hate!*

But Mowgli had to learn a great deal more than this. He didn't have the instinct of the jungle animals. He couldn't smell the predators coming his way. He couldn't run like the cheetah or climb like the monkey. He needed to learn all he could so he could compete against the rest of the jungle.

The boy could climb almost as well as he could swim, and could swim almost as well as he could run. So Baloo taught him the Wood and Water Laws, too. Mowgli learned how to speak politely to a hive of wild bees, what to say to Mang the bat when he disturbed him in the middle of the day, and how to warn the water-snakes in the pools before he splashed down among them. Baloo also taught Mowgli the Stranger's Hunting Call. This was to be repeated over and over until it was answered whenever one of the jungle animals hunted outside his own ground. It meant: "Allow me to hunt here because I am hungry." And the answer was: "Hunt then for food, but not for pleasure."

Mowgli had much to learn, and Bagheera worried about the rough way in which Baloo taught him.

"A man cub is a man cub and he must learn all the Law of the Jungle!" Baloo said to the panther one day. "Show him, Mowgli, what you have learned." The bear gave the boy a swat to the head with his paw. It wasn't meant to hurt, just to get his attention and let the boy know it was time to be serious.

The tired boy had worked for hours, and his head was ringing like a bee-tree. But he was happy to show off what he had learned. The answers to the questions flew from his lips as quickly as Baloo could ask.

"Now," said Baloo, "neither snake, bird, nor

beast would hurt him. He has only to fear his own tribe."

Mowgli had been trying to show off a bit — pulling at Bagheera's fur and kicking him. "Someday I shall have a tribe of my own and lead them through the jungle all day long. I shall make them do whatever I please."

"What is this fantasy, little dreamer of dreams?" said Bagheera with a laugh.

"I will throw branches and dirt at old Baloo," Mowgli continued.

Whoof! Baloo's big paw quickly scooped Mowgli up, letting the boy know the bear was angry.

"Mowgli," said Baloo, "you have been talking with the Monkey Folk, haven't you?"

Mowgli looked at Bagheera to see if the panther was angry, too. Bagheera's eyes were as hard as stones.

"You have been with the Monkey Folk—the gray apes—the people without a Law—the eaters of everything. That is very wrong!" the panther said.

"Baloo got mad at me one day and hurt my head," said Mowgli. "The gray apes came down from the trees and felt bad for me. No one else cared." He sniffled a little. "They gave me nuts and good things to eat, and they carried me in their arms to the top of the trees. They said I was their blood brother, except that I have no tail. They said I should be their leader someday."

"They have *no* leader," said Bagheera. "They lie. They have always lied."

"They were very kind and told me to come again. Why have I never been taken to them? The Monkey Folk stand on their feet as I do. They do not hit me with hard paws. They play all day. I want to play with them again!"

"Listen, man cub," said the bear. His voice rumbled like thunder on a hot night. "I have taught you the Laws of the Jungle for all the animals of the jungle—except for the Monkey Folk who live in the trees. They have no Law. They are not liked by anyone. They have no speech of their own. They listen to how we talk and steal our words. They are not leaders. They cannot remember things. They brag and chatter and pretend they are great animals about to do great things, but then a nut falls and their minds turn to laughter and all is forgotten. We of the jungle have nothing to do with them. We do not drink where the monkeys drink, we do not go where the monkeys go, we do not hunt where they hunt, and we do not die where they die. Have you ever heard me talk of the monkeys until today?"

"No," said Mowgli in a whisper, for the forest was now very still since Baloo had finished.

"The animals in the jungle put them out of

their minds. The Monkey Folk are evil and dirty. All they want is for the jungle animals to notice them. But we do not notice them, even when they throw nuts and dirt on our heads."

Baloo had barely finished talking when a shower of nuts and twigs fluttered down through the branches. They could hear coughing and howling and angry monkeys jumping high up in the thin branches above.

A fresh shower came down on their heads, and Baloo, Bagheera, and Mowgli walked away. What Baloo had said about the monkeys was true. They belonged to the treetops. Since the other jungle animals didn't live up there, they didn't see one another very often. But when the monkeys found a sick wolf, or a wounded tiger or bear, they bothered the beast by throwing sticks and nuts at him for fun.

When the Monkey Folk heard how angry Baloo was with Mowgli, they came up with the great idea to put Mowgli in their tribe. They knew he could weave sticks together for protection from the wind. If they caught him, he could teach them all how to do it. This time, they said, they were really going to have a leader and become the wisest people in the jungle. Then everyone else would notice them.

So they very quietly followed Baloo and Bagheera and Mowgli through the jungle until it was time for the midday nap. Mowgli snuggled in between Baloo and Bagheera, promising never to play with the Monkey Folk again.

The next thing Mowgli remembered was feeling hands on his legs and arms, and branches flying in his face. Two of the strongest monkeys caught Mowgli and swung off with him through the treetops. The boy couldn't help but enjoy the excitement of it all. The longer the game went on, however, the less fun it became. Mowgli began to grow angry. He wanted to tell Baloo and Bagheera

he was okay. He saw nothing as he looked down but the thickness of leaves and branches. When he looked up, he saw Chil the kite gliding in large circles as he kept watch over the jungle.

"Tell Baloo of the Seeonee Pack and Bagheera of the Council Rock that I am here!" Mowgli yelled as he swung through the air.

Chil nodded and rose up, watching Mowgli until he was out of sight.

By this time, Baloo and Bagheera were quite angry. They had tried to chase the boy for a bit, but the branches broke beneath them and the monkeys quickly outran them above.

"Why didn't you warn the man cub?" Bagheera roared at poor Baloo. "In all your teachings, why did you skip the lesson on the monkeys?"

Baloo clasped his paws over his ears and rolled over and over. "I am a fool," he moaned.

After a moment, he calmed down and said, "Hathi the wild elephant says everyone is afraid of something. He says the monkeys are afraid of Kaa the rock snake. Just the whisper of his name makes their tails cold. We must go see Kaa!"

"What will he do for us?" Bagheera asked.

"He is very old and wise. And he is always hungry. We can promise him many goats for his help!"

"He sleeps for a month after he eats," Bagheera said. "He may be asleep now."

"Then together we will see," said Baloo. And they went off to look for Kaa the rock python.

They found him stretched out on a warm ledge in the afternoon sun. He was staring at his beautiful new coat. He had been changing his skin for the last ten days, and now he was splendid. He twisted his head along the ground, moving the thirty feet of his body into wonderful knots and curves. He licked his lips as he thought about his dinner to come.

"He has not eaten," said Baloo with a smile when he saw the new skin. "He won't eat for a day or two after getting it. But be careful, Bagheera! He is always a little blind after he has changed his skin, and very quick to bite."

Kaa was not a poisonous snake. What made him harmful was his hug. When he wrapped his large body around something, there was no more to be said.

"Hello!" Baloo yelled to Kaa. "Good hunting!"

"Oh, Baloo, what are you doing here? Good hunting, Bagheera! Is there any news of food around here? A deer, perhaps? I am quite hungry!"

"We are hunting," said Baloo casually. He knew he never should hurry Kaa. He was too big.

"May I come with you?" Kaa asked. "It takes me forever to get my food! You are quick. On my last hunt, I came very near to falling off a cliff. The noise of my slipping woke the monkeys, and they called me bad names."

Baloo and Bagheera could tell the snake was angry.

"When I came up into the sun today," said Kaa, "I heard them whooping among the treetops."

"They have stolen our man cub!" said Bagheera quickly. "The best and wisest and bravest of man cubs . . ."

"We love him, Kaa," said Baloo.

Kaa shook his head back and forth before he spoke. "I also have known what love is. I can tell you many stories . . ."

"Not now, please," said Bagheera. "Our man cub is in the hands of the Monkey Folk. We know everyone fears Kaa the snake."

"They fear me and they have good reason," said Kaa. "Now, where did they take him?"

Baloo looked up as the cry of Chil the kite grew near. "I have seen Mowgli. He wants me to tell you! The monkeys have taken him beyond the river to the monkey city—to the Cold Lairs."

The Cold Lairs was an old, abandoned city. It was lost and buried in the jungle.

"Thank you, Chil," Baloo called. The old bear smiled, proud of Mowgli for using the bird to get a message to them.

Bagheera and Kaa quickly went on ahead to

the Cold Lairs. Baloo, who moved more slowly, followed, trying to make his own good time.

The monkeys had already arrived at the Cold Lairs. Now they were racing through the city, playing and laughing, having a great time. Mowgli, on the other hand, was not so happy.

"I am hungry," he said. "I am a stranger to this part of the jungle. Bring me food, or let me roam free to hunt."

The monkeys leapt away, promising to bring back food. But once they were on their way, they started to fight and ate some of the fruit intended for the boy. And so Mowgli ended up sore and angry as well as hungry. And now the night was falling as well.

All that Baloo said about the Monkey Folk is true, Mowgli thought. *They have no Law, no Hunting Call, and no leaders—nothing but foolish words and little hands that steal. If I am starved or killed here, it will be my own fault. I must find a way to return to the jungle.*

No sooner had Mowgli walked to the city wall than the monkeys pulled him back. They gathered around the boy and told him how great and wise and strong and gentle they were, and how foolish he was to wish to leave them. Mowgli laughed to himself, thinking of their silly ways.

Mowgli stood as quietly as he could, listening for a chance to get away. He didn't know that Kaa and Bagheera were nearby and ready to help him. The two walked near the back of the group of monkeys, allowing the darkness to hide them. But just as the black of night helps, it also can hurt. Bagheera tripped over the bodies of some monkeys, allowing himself to be known.

The monkeys grabbed the panther and began biting and scratching and tearing at his skin. Many more took hold of Mowgli and pushed him off the wall where he stood. The boy picked himself up and began fighting off the apes hanging on his back. Monkey Folk came from everywhere to help their brothers. Bagheera and Baloo, who had finally made his way to the Cold Lairs, both received many hits trying to keep their young friend safe. It took a long, slithering push of twelve monkeys or more, from Kaa the snake, before the fight began to slow down. "Kaa! It's Kaa! Run! Run!" the monkeys called.

Kaa was everything the monkeys feared in the jungle. No one ever came out of his hug alive. And so they ran.

By the end of the battle, Mowgli and his friends were tired, sore, and ready to leave.

"Jump on my back, Little Brother," said Bagheera, "and we will go home."

Mowgli laid his head on Bagheera's back and slept deeply. He didn't even wake when Bagheera put him down by Mother Wolf's side in the home cave to dream of better things.

CHAPTER 3

"Tiger! Tiger!"

⁓

Now we must go back to the first story. When Mowgli left the wolves' cave after the fight with the Pack at the Council Rock, he took the road past the jungle and down into the valley. At one end stood a little village; at the other end, the thick jungle began. Cattle and buffalo were grazing over all the fields. When the little boys in charge of the herds saw Mowgli, they shouted and ran away. But Mowgli was very hungry, so he continued walking toward the village. Finally he arrived at a gate that was pushed open to one side.

Mowgli sat down by the gate. A man came out, and the boy stood up, opened his mouth, and pointed at it to show that he wanted food. The man stared for a moment, then ran back up the street of the village shouting for the priest. The priest was a big, fat man dressed in white, with a red-and-yellow mark on his forehead. He came to the gate, and with him at least a hundred people. The group stared and talked and shouted and pointed at Mowgli.

"He is a wolf child!" the priest said. "Look at the scars on his arms and legs."

"He is a handsome boy," said two or three women together. "He has eyes like red fire. He looks like the boy that was taken by the tiger!"

"Let me look," said a woman with lots of jewels around her neck and wrists. "He is thinner, but he has the very look of my boy, my Nathoo."

The priest was a smart man and knew that this woman, Messua, was the wife of the richest man in the village. "The jungle has taken from you, but it has also given back. Take this boy home tonight."

All this talking is like being looked over by the Pack! Mowgli thought. *Well, if I am a man, a man I must become.*

The woman with the jewels took Mowgli to her hut. She gave him food and drink and talked to him in a language he couldn't understand.

For the next few hours, Mowgli imitated the words he heard almost perfectly. By the end of the day, he had learned the names of many things in the hut. At bedtime, though, Mowgli was afraid to stay inside. He had never slept in a house. When Messua's husband shut the door, Mowgli crawled out through the window.

This upset Messua, but her husband said, "Remember, if he is really sent in the place of our son, he will not run away."

So Mowgli stretched himself out in some long, clean grass at the edge of the field. But when he closed his eyes, a soft gray nose poked him under the chin.

"Phew!" said Gray Brother (he was the oldest of Mother Wolf's cubs). "You smell like wood smoke and cattle! Wake up, Little Brother. I bring you news!"

"All are well in the jungle?" asked Mowgli.

"All except the wolves who were burned by the Red Flower. I have come to tell you that Shere Khan has gone away to hunt until his fur grows in. You have not forgotten you are a wolf, have you?" asked Gray Brother.

"Never. I will always remember my love for everyone in our cave. But I need to remember, too, that I was thrown out of the Pack."

"You may be thrown out of another pack as well, Little Brother. Men are only men," Gray Brother said and left, leaving Mowgli confused again about where he belonged.

Three months passed, and Mowgli hardly ever left the village. He was busy learning the ways of men. First he had to wear a cloth around him, which bothered him terribly. Then he had to learn about money and plowing fields. The little children in the village made him very angry. They made fun of him for not understanding how to play their games or fly kites. They often teased him about the way he spoke, too.

The one thing that Mowgli did do well was use his strength. He was quickly chosen by the men as a buffalo herder. With this job, he was allowed to sit with the village club each evening under the great fig tree. This group was made up of the most respected men in the village. The headman and the watchman who were in charge of making decisions and keeping the village safe were the leaders of the group. The barber (who knew all the gossip of the village) and old Buldeo, the village hunter, were there, too. The men talked about everything imaginable. They told stories to the villagers of gods and men and ghosts. Buldeo told even more wonderful stories of the animals in the jungle—so wonderful that the eyes of the children sitting outside the circle seemed to nearly pop out of their heads. He explained that the tiger had carried away Messua's son. He called it a ghost-tiger, probably because of its light coloring.

Mowgli, who knew what the animals were really like, had to cover his face to hide his laughter.

Buldeo was shocked to see the boy act in this way.

"Oh, it is the jungle brat. If you know so much about animals, bring the tiger here. The government will give you money for his life."

Mowgli rose to go. "All evening I have been listening to your stories. And Buldeo has said only one or two things about the jungle that are true."

"It is time you left for your work," Buldeo snorted at Mowgli, angry at being called a liar.

In most Indian villages, the boys take the cattle and buffalo out to graze in the early morning and bring them back at night. Mowgli was the master of his group, and told one of the boys to graze the cattle while he went on with the herd. Mowgli drove them on to the edge of the plain, where the river came out of the jungle. Here he found Gray Brother.

"Ah!" said Gray Brother. "I have waited for many days. What is the meaning of this cattle-herding work?"

"It is an order," said Mowgli. "I am a village herder for a while. What news do you have of Shere Khan?"

"He is hunting for you," said Gray Brother.

"While Shere Khan is away, you or one of my brothers shall sit on that rock so that I can see you as I come out of the village each day," Mowgli told him. "When he comes back, wait for me in the ditch by the tall tree in the center of the plain. That way I will know when he is there and waiting for me."

Day after day, Mowgli led the buffalo out to the fields, and day after day he saw his brothers in the same place. At last the day came when he did not see Gray Brother there. He herded the buffalo toward the ditch by the tall tree in the center of the plain, and there sat Gray Brother.

"Shere Khan and Tabaqui are coming," the wolf said with fear.

Mowgli frowned. "I am not afraid of Shere Khan, but Tabaqui can be very sneaky."

Gray Brother answered, "Shere Khan's plan is to wait for you at the village gate tonight."

"Has he eaten anything today, or is he hunting hungry?" Mowgli asked, for the answer to this could mean life or death to him.

"He ate this morning," said Gray Brother.

Mowgli smiled. "He couldn't even wait for me."

Gray Brother looked at him thoughtfully. "I have brought a wise helper."

Mowgli followed Gray Brother to a hole where a huge gray head was poking up.

"Akela! Akela!" said Mowgli, clapping his hands. "I should have guessed you wouldn't forget me. We have big work ahead of us. Help me divide the buffalo and cattle herds in half."

Within minutes, Gray Brother and Akela had split the herds.

"Drive the bulls away to the left, Akela," said Mowgli. "Gray Brother, you go to the right. When you two meet, drive them into the ditch. Take them in until the sides of the cliff are higher than Shere Khan can jump. Keep them there until we come down. Go now!"

Mowgli's plan was simple. He would lead Shere Khan into the ditch, and then escape up the side, leaving the tiger trapped between the buffalo and the cows. He knew there was no way the tiger could fight or clamber up the sides of the ditch on a full stomach.

When the plan started, the boy yelled for the tiger. He got as close to Shere Khan as he could without getting caught in the herd himself. "Ha! Ha!" said Mowgli when Shere Khan was trapped. "Now you know who finishes our fight!"

Mowgli heard an answering cry from the bottom of the ditch. The buffalo and cattle, who were confused about which way to move, were now ramming into one another and running back and forth.

Mowgli pictured Shere Khan in the ditch, pacing back and forth, too heavy with his breakfast and drink to run. He would look to the sides, hoping to find a way to escape. Not wanting to move any more than necessary after his big meal, the tiger would be willing to do anything other than fight.

Mowgli watched the large group of animals and saw the frightened creatures growing upset.

"Quick, Akela! Break them up! Scatter them or they will hurt one another. It's all over."

Akela and Gray Brother ran through the crowd of animals, nipping the legs of the beasts to turn them around. When the ground finally cleared, the body of the tiger lay motionless. Shere Khan was dead.

"We must get to work quickly," Mowgli said, pulling a knife from his pocket. Taking the hide of the tiger would be hard work.

"You are stupid and lucky," came a voice from behind the boy. It was Buldeo. The children of the village had told him about the buffalo stampede, and Buldeo had come to scold Mowgli. "That tiger just ate, or he would have run twenty miles from here by now. You can't even catch him the right way, you little beggar brat. I will take the hide myself, and I won't give you one cent of the reward."

"Must I listen to you babble all day?" Mowgli said. "Akela, this man is bothering me."

Before he knew what was happening, Buldeo found himself flat out on the ground, with Akela growling over him. Mowgli simply continued to skin the tiger.

"I'm sorry," said Buldeo. "I didn't know you were able to . . . May I leave, or will this wolf tear me to pieces?"

"Go!" said Mowgli. "And peace go with you. But next time, stay out of my way!"

Buldeo raced back to his village and told a story of magic. The boy was skinning the large tiger of the jungle while the leader of the Wolf Pack looked on!

Meanwhile, Mowgli and the two wolves trotted toward the hill of the Council Rock. Before they reached it, though, they stopped at Mother Wolf's cave.

"They will make me leave the Man Pack, Mother," said Mowgli, "but I have brought the hide of Shere Khan like I promised."

Mother Wolf's eyes glowed when she saw the skin. "I knew the day would come when the hunter would be hunted. It is finally done."

"Little Brother, it is well done," said a deep voice in the bushes. "We were lonely in the jungle without you." Bagheera came running to Mowgli. They climbed up the Council Rock together, and Mowgli spread the skin out on the flat stone where Akela used to sit.

The many wolves of the Pack gathered around. The Pack had been without a leader since Akela had left. Many were hurt from fights, limping from traps, or sick from eating bad food.

"I have kept my word to you!" said Mowgli. "I bring you the hide of the tiger."

The rumble of voices filled the crowd. "Lead us again, Akela! Lead us again, man cub! We are sick of no Laws. We want to be free animals once more!"

"No," said Mowgli. I have been thrown out of the Pack. I will hunt in the jungle alone."

"And we will hunt with you," said the four cubs of Mother Wolf.

So Mowgli went away, and from that day on he hunted with the four cubs. But he was not always alone, because years afterward he became a man and married. But that is a story for grown-ups.

CHAPTER 4

How Fear Came

✧

Mowgli spent a great part of his life in the Seeonee Wolf Pack, learning the Law of the Jungle from Baloo. And it was the brown bear who told him that everyone in the jungle obeys at least one Law.

This talk went in one ear and out the other. Mowgli didn't worry about anything until it was actually staring him in the face. But one year, before he killed Shere Khan, Baloo's words came true, and Mowgli saw all the jungle working under the one Law.

It began when the winter rains didn't come. Ikki, the porcupine, told Mowgli that the wild yams were drying up. Mowgli knew the porcupine sometimes told little white lies, so the boy asked, "What is that to me?"

"Not much *now,*" said Ikki, straightening his quills. "But later we shall see. Are you going to dive again into the deep rock pool below the Bee-Rocks?"

"No. The water is all dried up," said Mowgli.

"That is your loss," said Ikki. He moved away from the man cub and allowed Baloo to step in.

"If I were alone," said Baloo, "I would change my hunting grounds now, before the others figure out what is going on. And yet, I would hate to hunt among strangers. That can only lead to fighting. And they could hurt my man cub. We will have to wait and see how the mohwa blooms."

That spring, the mohwa tree that Baloo was so fond of never flowered. The heat killed the green-and-white blossoms before they were born. Only a few bad-smelling petals came down when he shook the tree.

As time went on, the heat seeped into the heart of the jungle. The green slowly turned to brown, as the trees and grass burned up. The pools of water from rain dried up. The moss peeled off the rocks until they were bare and hot in the sun.

Mowgli, who had never known what real hunger meant, lived on stale honey, three years old, scraped out of old rock hives. He hunted, too, for grubs under the bark of trees. The animals in the jungle were no more than skin and bone. Bagheera could kill all night and hardly get a full meal. But the thirst for water was the worst.

The heat went on and on, drying up everything, until at last the main river of the Waingunga was the only stream that carried a trickle of water. Hathi, the wild elephant who had lived for a hundred years and more, saw a long strip of rock in the very center of the stream. He knew that he was looking at the Peace Rock. It had been given its name years ago for the peace made there by all the animals of the jungle. Then and there Hathi lifted up his trunk and announced a Water Truce, just as his father had done fifty years ago. By the Law of the Jungle, the Water Truce meant that any animal could go to the stream for a drink without fearing that he would be hurt by another animal. So, starved and weary, to the small stream they came—tiger, bear, deer, buffalo, and pig, all together—to drink the water they found.

It was here that Mowgli came nightly now, for the cool and the friendship. The young boy was hard to recognize. His hair was white from the sun; his ribs stood out like the weaving of a basket. The lumps on his knees and elbows looked like roots of grass stems. But his eyes were cool and quiet.

"It is an evil time," said Bagheera one extra-hot night. "But it will be fine for us if we can make it to the end. Is your stomach full, Mowgli?"

"There is food in my stomach, but I get nothing from it. Do you think, Bagheera, that the rains have forgotten us and will never come again?"

"Not I!" said Bagheera. "We shall see the mohwa in blossom again, and the little fawns all fat with new grass. Come down to the Peace Rock and hear the news. On my back, Little Brother!"

The tall jungle grass around the stream stood dead and dying. The tracks of deer and pigs heading toward the river had beaten it down. When they reached the Peace Rock, Mowgli and Bagheera could see the other animals taking their drinks to stay alive.

"We are under one Law, that is certain!" said Bagheera as he waded into the water and looked at the different animals across the stream from him. The deer and the pigs were pushing one another while the elephant let a snoutful of water spray from his trunk. The tension among the animals was easy to see.

"If it weren't for the Law of the Jungle," said Bagheera, "we would have some mighty fine hunting here."

The deer drinking nearby heard the last sentence, and a frightened whisper started to spread among them. "The Truce! Remember the Truce!" they cried.

"I remember!" said Bagheera lazily, rolling his eyes upstream. "I eat turtles—and frogs. Why do you worry?"

The talk among the animals went back to normal. They spoke of the roaring hot wind, the scattered twigs, and the dust on the water. Baloo wandered into the group, listening to the serious conversation of the animals.

"You know," said a young deer, "the menfolk, too, are dying beside their plows. I passed three just today. They lie still, and their ox with them. Soon it shall be us lying still."

"The river has fallen since last night," said Baloo, wanting to add what he knew. "Hathi, have you ever seen a drought this bad?"

"It will pass, it will pass," said Hathi.

"We have one here who can't make it much longer," said Baloo, pointing to the boy he loved.

Suddenly the eyes of the animals shifted. Shere Khan was limping toward the water. The tiger walked slowly, enjoying the cries of fright from the deer on the bank.

"What brings you here with that look of evil in your eyes?" said Bagheera, asking what all the other animals were afraid to ask.

The limping tiger had dipped his chin in the water for a drink. Dark oily streaks floated downstream from his face.

"I just killed a man an hour ago," Shere Khan said, purring and growling to himself.

The line of animals shook with fear and anger.
Whispers grew into cries. "Man! Man! He has
killed Man!"

They all looked toward Hathi, the wild elephant, but he seemed not to hear.

"Wasn't there anything else you could eat?"
Bagheera asked, stepping back from the water.

"Of course," said Shere Khan. "But I chose to
eat Man."

Bagheera's fur went up in anger. Hathi lifted
up his trunk and spoke quietly.

"The kill was your choice?" he asked.

"Yes," said the tiger. "It was my right."

"I know it was. Have you had enough water?"
Hathi asked.

"For tonight, yes," answered Shere Khan.

"Go then. The river is for drinking. No one
but you would stand here bragging about eating
while the rest of us are starving! Leave now!" said
Hathi.

The words rang out like trumpets. Shere Khan slipped away, not daring to growl. He knew what everyone else knew—that Hathi was the Master of the Jungle and must be obeyed.

"I don't understand," said Mowgli. "Hathi, what is Shere Khan's right?"

All the animals on the banks stopped to listen, for they, too, wanted to understand what was meant by the tiger's right.

"It is an old story," said Hathi. "A story older than the jungle. Keep quiet along the banks and I will tell the tale.

"You know," he began softly, "the thing you all fear the most is Man."

The crowd of animals nodded in agreement.

"But do you know why you fear Man?" Hathi asked. "This is the reason. In the beginning of the jungle, all animals walked together. We had no fear of one another. In those days there was plenty of rain, which meant no drought. There were leaves and flowers and fruit all on the same tree. We ate nothing at all except leaves and flowers and grass and fruit and bark."

"I am glad I was not born in those days," said Bagheera.

"Back then, the Lord of the Jungle was Tha, the First of the Elephants," Hathi continued. "He made the jungles himself. He made ditches in the ground with his tusks, and there the rivers ran. Where he stomped his foot, great ponds of water lay. When he blew through his trunk, the trees fell. That was how he made the jungles.

"In those days there was no corn or melon or pepper or sugar. There were no little huts. And the jungle animals knew nothing about Man. But soon they began to fight over their food, even though there was enough grazing for all. They were lazy. Each wanted to sleep right where he ate."

Hathi took a breath and continued. "Well, Tha

couldn't do everything. He couldn't make the jungles *and* take care of all the animals, so he named the First of the Tigers the Master of the Jungle. It was to this great yellow animal that the animals could take their problems. Now, in those days the tigers ate fruit and grass with the others. We were all the same. But one night, there was an argument between two deer. The First of the Tigers forgot that he was the Master of the Jungle. He got in the middle of the fight and killed one of the deer."

The crowd of animals was very quiet as they listened to the story.

"Until that night, no animal had ever died. Seeing what he had done, the First of the Tigers ran away into the jungle in shame. Without a judge to settle their problems, the rest of the animals started fighting among themselves. They still needed a Master of the Jungle, but the only one who wanted the job was the gray ape. Now, children, you know the gray ape. He was the same then as he is now. At first he tried to be very wise, but in a little while he started his silly ways: scratching, hanging upside down, and leaping through the trees. And so there was no Law in the jungle—only foolish talk and nonsense words.

"Then Tha called the animals together and told them that there needed to be a Law that none of them would break. First, they were to find Fear. When they had found it, they would know that it was their master and would follow it.

"The buffalo found it first. They came back with the news that in a cave in the jungle sat Fear. He had no hair and stood up on his hind legs. The animals followed the herd of buffalo back to the cave and found the beast standing there. He growled at them, and his voice scared the animals so badly that they ran away, trampling upon one another. That night, the animals of the jungle did not lie together as usual. Each tribe went off alone — the pig with the pig, the deer with the deer — all lay shaking in the jungle.

"Only the First of the Tigers was not with them, for he was still hidden in the tall grass. When he found out about the Thing the animals had seen in the cave, he said, 'I will go to this Thing and kill it.' So he ran all night until he reached the cave. But the trees on his path remembered what Tha had said about looking for Fear, and they let down their branches to scratch the tiger as he ran by. Wherever they touched him, they left a mark and a stripe on his yellow fur. By the end of his run, the tiger had marks all over his body. And to this day, his children still wear those stripes!

"When the tiger got to the cave, Fear put his hand out and called him 'the Striped One That Comes by Night.' But the First of the Tigers was so afraid of the Hairless One that he ran back to the tall grasses, howling."

Mowgli chuckled quietly, his chin in the water.

"He cried so loud that Tha heard him and asked him what was wrong. The First of the Tigers lifted his head and said, 'Give me back my power, Tha. I am shamed in front of all the animals. I have run away from the Hairless One, and he has called me an ugly name. I am marked with the mud of the marshes.'

"Tha answered, 'Swim then, and roll on the wet grass, and if it is mud, it will wash away.'

"The First of the Tigers did as he was told, swimming and rolling upon the green grass until he was dizzy. But not one little bar of black on him was changed.

"Then the First of the Tigers said, 'What have I done to deserve this?'

"Tha answered, 'You have killed a buck and let death into the jungle. And with death comes fear.'

"'The other animals will never fear me,' the First of the Tigers said. 'I have known them from the beginning.'

"'Go and see if that is true,' answered Tha.

"The tiger left, calling aloud to the pig and the deer and all the animals of the jungle. But they all ran away from him, afraid, as Tha had said.

"The First of the Tigers came back. His head hung low and he tore up the dirt in anger. 'Remember, I was once the Master of the Jungle. Don't forget me, Tha!'

"And Tha said, 'Since I have known you so long, I shall make you a deal. For one night in each year, it will be like it was before the buck was killed. In that one night, if you meet the Hairless One—and his name is Man—you will not be afraid of him. He will be afraid of you. Show him kindness in that night of fear, for you know what fear is.'

"Then the First of the Tigers answered, 'Yes, that will do.' But when he drank from the water, he saw the black stripes on his back and side shining back at him. He remembered what the Hairless One had called him, and this made him angry. But he held in his anger until the night came when he was to meet the Hairless One. It happened just as Tha had told him. When the First of the Tigers jumped upon the Hairless One, the Tiger felt he had killed Fear. He proudly told Tha of his work.

"'You blind and foolish Tiger!' Tha said. 'You have only taught Man to kill!'

"The First of the Tigers stood in surprise. 'But it is just the same as when I killed the buck. There is no more Fear.'

"'Killing one is not killing Fear,' Tha answered. 'You have only killed one of many of them. The

Hairless Ones will follow you now. They will set traps to catch you and fill your paths with things to make you fall. You have shown them no kindness and they will show you none, either.'

"So the day came when another Hairless One saw the First of the Tigers, and he took a pointed stick and threw it, sticking the tiger deep in his body. Now all the jungle knew that the Hairless One could hit from far off, and they feared him more than before. And now we know the harm that the Tiger did by teaching the Hairless One to kill. For the rest of the year, Fear walks up and down the jungle by day and by night. But for one night in the year, the Hairless One is afraid of the tiger, as Tha promised. And the tiger always reminds him to be afraid."

"Ahhh!" said the deer, thinking of what the story meant to them.

"Only when there is one great Fear over all, as there is now with no rain, can we put aside our little fears and meet together in one place as we do today."

"For one night only does Man fear the tiger?" asked Mowgli.

"For one night only," said Hathi.

"But everyone knows Shere Khan kills Man on more than one night," said Mowgli.

"Yes," said Hathi, "but he springs from behind and turns his head when he attacks. He is full of fear as he does it. If a man looked at him, he would run. But on his one night, he goes down through the village like a king and chooses his victim."

"Does the Tiger know which night this will be?" asked Bagheera.

"Not until the Jackal of the Moon stands clearly in the evening mist."

The deer made sorrowful sounds and Bagheera smiled wickedly, thinking of that night. It reminded him of how much he enjoyed a good meal.

"Do men know this tale?" he asked.

"No one knows it except the tigers and us, the children of Tha."

Hathi dipped his trunk into the water as a sign that he did not wish to talk anymore.

"But why didn't the First of the Tigers continue to eat grass and leaves and trees?" asked Mowgli, turning to Baloo. "He did not eat the deer."

"The trees and bushes marked him and made him striped," said Baloo. "He never again ate fruit, but he did eat the animals who were the eaters of the grass."

"Why have I never heard this story?" asked Mowgli.

"Because the jungle is full of these stories. If I made a beginning, there would never be an end."

Baloo took a breath and looked at his listeners. "But that, my children, is the end of stories for this day."

CHAPTER 5

Letting in the Jungle

∽

You will remember that after Mowgli laid Shere Khan's fur on the Council Rock, he told the Seeonee Pack that from then on he would hunt in the jungle alone. The four children of Mother and Father Wolf said they would hunt with him. But it is not easy to change your life in a minute—especially in the jungle. The first thing Mowgli did when the Pack wandered off was go to his home cave and sleep for a day and a night. Then he told Mother and Father

Wolf as much as he could about his adventures living among men. The stories made his mother upset.

"I am glad I did not see the poor way they treated you," said Mother Wolf sadly.

"Leave men alone," said Father Wolf.

Baloo and Bagheera both answered back, "Leave men alone!"

Mowgli put his head on Mother Wolf's side and smiled. "I never want to see, hear, or smell men again."

"But what if men don't leave you alone, Little Brother?" asked Akela.

"Then we will help Mowgli!" snapped Gray Brother.

"Little Brother," continued Akela, "a man with a gun is following our path now. And men do not carry guns for fun."

"But why? The men have already thrown me

out of their group. What more do they need?" Mowgli asked, his voice full of anger.

"You are a man, Little Brother," Akela said. "You should know the answer, not us."

All of a sudden Akela sat up and stared into the distance.

"Man!" he growled.

The four cubs said nothing, but ran down the hill on their bellies. Mowgli followed, cutting through the jungle until he came upon Buldeo in the distance. The man was tired and ready for a rest. A group of other men came down the path and joined him. The gathering of men talked for some time, and Buldeo made up stories of how he had killed Shere Khan himself. He said Mowgli had turned into a wolf and killed one of Buldeo's buffalo. The villagers had declared Buldeo the bravest hunter and told him to go out and find Mowgli. While he did this, the village would keep

Messua and her husband locked in their own hut
so they couldn't protect their son.

"I am going to go back to the Man Pack,"
Mowgli said.

"What about this group of men?" Gray
Brother asked.

"I don't want them at the village gates until it
is dark," Mowgli answered. "Can you hold them
here?"

"We can lead them around in circles like
goats," Gray Brother replied, laughing.

"Don't do that," Mowgli said. "Just lead them
on with a sweet song. Bagheera, go with them.
When the night is over, meet me by the village.
Gray Brother knows the place."

The man cub left the group to go about their
work. He had his own job to do. His first wish was
to get Messua and her husband out of their hut.
Mowgli didn't reach the village until it was almost
dark. Angry as he was at the actions of the men,

something jumped in Mowgli's throat and he had to catch his breath when he looked into the village. Everyone had come in from the fields early. Instead of cooking their evening meal, they were gathered in a crowd, chattering and shouting.

Mowgli crept around the outside wall of the village until he came to Messua's hut. He looked through the window into the room. There lay Messua, tied up with a rope. She had a handkerchief tied around her mouth. She was breathing hard and groaning. Her husband was tied up as well. The front door of the hut was shut tight. Three or four people were sitting with their backs to it, guarding the door.

Mowgli knew that Buldeo would be coming soon, with a mighty fine story to tell. He would have to work quickly. He crawled through a window and stooped over the man and woman to cut the ropes and handkerchiefs.

Messua was half wild with pain and fear. "I

knew you would come!" she sobbed. "Now I *know* that you are my son!" She hugged the boy hard.

Until this time, Mowgli had been perfectly calm. Now he began to shake all over, and that surprised him greatly.

"Why are you tied?" Mowgli asked the question he had been wondering for quite some time.

"For having you as our son," said the man softly. "Look! We bleed!"

Mowgli looked at Messua and gritted his teeth when he saw the blood.

"Who did this to you?" he demanded. "I will get them for this!"

"It was the work of the entire village," said Messua's husband. "We aren't poor like many of the other villagers. We have money and cattle. We could afford to give a young boy a home. But they call us witches because we opened our doors to you."

"I don't understand," said Mowgli. "Let Messua tell the story."

"I gave you milk, don't you remember?" Messua said in a quiet voice. "Because you were my son, whom the tiger took, and because I loved you dearly. They said I was the mother of a crazy child, and must therefore be punished."

"You are not crazy," the man said. "But that will not help us. We cannot stay here. What should we do?"

"The road to the jungle is just over there," Mowgli said, pointing through the window. "Your hands and feet are free. Go now!"

"We don't know the jungle as you do, my son," Messua said. "And I don't think I could walk far."

"The men would catch us and bring us back here anyway," her husband said.

Mowgli thought out loud. "I have no wish to harm the villagers, at least not right now. But I

don't think you will be safe here for very long.
Ah!" He lifted his head and listened to shouting
and trampling outside. "The wolves have let
Buldeo come home at last!"

"He was sent out this morning to find you!"
Messua cried. "Did you meet him?"

"Yes, we—I—met him. He has a story to tell
the villagers. While he is telling it, there will be
time to do much. But first, I must know what
they mean to do to you. I will be back." Mowgli
leapt through the window and ran along the wall
of the village until he could hear the words coming from the crowd. Buldeo was lying on the
ground, coughing and groaning. Everyone was
asking him questions. His hair had fallen around
his shoulders, his hands and legs were skinned
from climbing up trees, and he could hardly talk.
He mumbled words about a wolf boy to interest
the crowd, and then called for water.

"Men are so dumb!" Mowgli whispered as he turned to run back to the hut. He knew no one would leave to check on Messua until they had heard Buldeo's stories.

Just as Mowgli was about to climb back through the window, he felt a touch on his foot.

"Mother Wolf," he said, for he knew her tongue well. "What are you doing here?"

"I would like to see the mother who first gave you milk," she said.

"They tied her up and tried to keep her from helping me. I cut her loose, but she must hide. She can run through the jungle with her man."

"I will follow her," Mother Wolf said as she stood to look in the window of the dark hut. "No one will hurt her."

She dropped back to the ground. Her face was sad. "Perhaps it is true. Man will always go back to Man."

"Maybe," said Mowgli. "But I am not thinking about that now. Stay down so Messua won't see you."

Mowgli swung into the hut again and told Messua and her husband what was happening. "The crowd of men is listening to Buldeo tell stories that never happened. When his talk is over, they will come here. They plan on burning the hut."

"I have spoken to my husband," said Messua. "Kanhiwara is thirty miles from here. There are good people there who do not harm others. If we can get there tonight, we will live. If not, we die."

Mowgli helped Messua and her husband out the window of the hut.

"Do you know the trail to Kanhiwara?" he whispered.

They nodded.

"Good. Remember not to be afraid. And there is no need to hurry. I will slow them on this end. Now go!"

Messua flung herself sobbing at Mowgli's feet, but he lifted her very quickly. She put her arms around his neck and called him every sweet name she could think of, until her husband called her away.

Messua and her husband went off toward the jungle, and Mother Wolf leapt from her place of hiding.

"Follow!" said Mowgli. "And make sure that all the jungle knows these two are safe. I will call Bagheera."

Not long after they left, Bagheera appeared out of the darkness at Mowgli's feet.

"I am glad you are here," Mowgli said. "Where are my brothers? I don't want any of the Man Pack to leave the gates tonight."

"What do you need the four cubs for?" asked Bagheera, his eyes blazing, purring louder and louder. "I can hold them, Little Brother! I am Bagheera—in the jungle—in the night, and all my strength is in me. Why, I could make a man flat as a dead frog with just one swipe of my paw!"

"Do it then!" shouted Mowgli. His loud, mean tone made Bagheera come to a full stop. He sat back on his hind legs and began to shake. Mowgli stared at the panther's green eyes until the cat lowered his gaze to the ground.

"I am sorry," Mowgli said. "Tonight is a hard night for us all."

Mowgli and the panther lay down, resting their minds and their legs.

"They are very long at their talk," Mowgli said, thinking of Buldeo and the villagers. "They should be here soon for the woman and man. Won't they be surprised to see that they are gone?"

"And who better to find in their place than *me*?" said the panther. "I don't think they would try to tie me up!"

Mowgli laughed. "Be careful then!"

The panther took his place in the hut while Mowgli waited outside. Within minutes, the crowd of villagers arrived.

"Burn the hut!" they cried.

The group pushed toward the door of the hut, tugging it until it came open. The light of the torches streamed into the room. There, stretched out on the bed, lay Bagheera—his paws crossed, dangling from the bed, black as the night. He yawned, showing his pink tongue against his sharp, white teeth.

In the next instant Bagheera leapt out the window. He stood at Mowgli's side while a yelling, screaming group of men tumbled over one another in their panic to get away and safely back to their own huts.

"They will not come out again until daylight," said Bagheera quietly.

"Watch the village until then. I will sleep," said Mowgli to the panther.

Mowgli fell asleep almost instantly across a rock in the jungle. He slept for hours, and when he awoke, Bagheera was at his side. A newly killed buck lay at his feet. Mowgli used his knife to cut the buck, then ate and drank as the panther watched.

"The man and woman are safe and very near Kanhiwara," Bagheera said. "The village didn't wake until the sun was up high this morning. Then they ate their food and ran quickly back to their houses."

"Did they see you?" Mowgli asked.

"Maybe," said the panther. "But what does it really matter, Little Brother? There is nothing more to do. Come hunting with me and Baloo. We want you back with us like in the old days. The man and woman are safe and all goes well in the jungle. Let's forget the Man Pack."

"In a while," said Mowgli. "First, send Hathi and his three sons to see me tonight. He knows of villages where Man has taken over."

Bagheera found the elephants, and together they went to see Mowgli. "What do you need?" asked Hathi.

"You know the village of the Man Pack that threw me out. They are mean and senseless. They kill for sport. They hurt one another. I have seen this with my own eyes. It is not good for them to be here anymore," said Mowgli.

"What shall we do?" Hathi asked, wondering why Mowgli had called for him.

"We need to let the jungle in upon the village," Mowgli said slowly.

Bagheera shivered. That was not what he would have done.

"Let the jungle in—let the men run as the men in other places have run from the fields, until we have enough rainwater on the leaves, until the bucks drink at the tank behind the temple. Let the jungle in, Hathi!"

It took days, but all the animals of the jungle joined in. The deer helped break down the dams, and the village flooded. Grazing grounds and crops were ruined. The wild pigs destroyed what the deer didn't get to. The men's last hope was to live on their stored corn seed until the rains came. But while the men were out working, Hathi's sharp tusks ripped open the corner of the mud house where the seed was stored. Now it was destroyed as well.

Thinking that the Gods of the Jungles were against them, the villagers gave up. The cries of the elephants and other animals no longer bothered them, for they had no more to be scared of.

The corn on the ground and the seed in the ground had been taken. The fields were already losing their shape. It was time for them to head for Kanhiwara.

As the last family moved out, they heard a crash of falling beams and walls. It was Hathi, pulling the roofs off their houses.

"The jungle will swallow these little huts," said a quiet voice.

"All in good time, Mowgli," Hathi replied. The father and his three sons pushed on the village wall until it split and fell. The villagers, watching in horror, ran down the valley crying as their homes fell down behind them.

A month later, the place was a small bump covered with soft green grass. By the end of the rainy season, no one ever would have guessed that a Man Pack had lived there just six months before.

CHAPTER 6

The King's Ankus

❦

Kaa, the big rock python, had changed his skin maybe two hundred times since he was born. Skin changing always made him grouchy and sad until the new skin began to shine and look beautiful.

Mowgli, who never forgot that the snake had saved his life at the Cold Lairs, decided to go and cheer him up. Kaa had learned to treat Mowgli as part of the jungle family. He enjoyed telling Mowgli stories. Snakes spend most of their time in the Middle Jungle, as Kaa called the area low to the ground. And the Middle Jungle was full of news.

"I need water," Kaa said. "A new skin never shines before the first bath. Let us go bathe."

The boy and the python had a great time wrestling about and racing in the water. They played for hours before climbing out onto the rocks to rest.

"This is very good," said Mowgli sleepily. "If I were in the Man Pack at this time of day, I would lie down upon a hard piece of wood in the middle of a hut. All the windows would be shut and cloths would cover us up. It is better in the jungle."

"So the jungle gives you everything you need, Little Brother?" Kaa asked.

"Not everything," said Mowgli, laughing. "I wish for sun on a rainy day, and food without having to chase and kill it, and a few other things."

"You want nothing else?" Kaa asked.

"What more can I wish for?" Mowgli answered with a smile.

"The cobra snake said——" Kaa began.

"What cobra?" asked Mowgli.

"Another snake I know," said Kaa quickly.

"Well, what did this snake say?" asked Mowgli with wonder.

"Three or four moons ago, I hunted in the Cold Lairs. The thing that I hunted ran screaming to his burrow."

"But the people of the Cold Lairs do not live in burrows." Mowgli knew that Kaa was talking of the Monkey Folk.

"This thing ran into a burrow that led very far. I followed, but soon became too tired. I slept, and when I woke, I went farther."

"Under the earth?" Mowgli asked.

"Yes," said Kaa. "And I came upon a white cobra. It talked about things I had never heard of before and showed me things I had never before seen."

"Was there new food?" Kaa asked.

"No, not new food," Kaa answered. "The white cobra said that a man would pay anything to see the things he showed me."

"We will look," said Mowgli, remembering that he had once been a man.

Kaa added, "The white cobra said it had been a long time since he had seen a man. If I knew one, I was to bring him and show him these things that are so important."

"Let us go!" said Mowgli, excited. The two set off for the Cold Lairs, the empty city of the Monkey Folk. Although Mowgli was not the least bit afraid of the Monkey Folk, they feared him with all their might. But their tribes were fighting in the jungle, and the city of Cold Lairs was empty and silent in the moonlight.

Kaa led the way underground. They crawled a

long way, down a sloping path that turned and twisted many times. At last they came to a place where the root of a giant tree had forced a stone out of the wall. They crept through the hole and found themselves in a large room where the roof had been broken away by tree roots. A few streaks of light shone down into the darkness.

"Now what?" Mowgli asked, standing up straight.

"Excuse me!" said a voice in the middle of the room. Mowgli saw something white move until, little by little, there stood the biggest cobra he had ever seen. He was nearly eight feet long and had eyes as red as rubies. Altogether he was a most wonderful and scary sight.

"Good hunting!" greeted Mowgli, using his manners.

"What do you think of my city?" the white cobra asked. "My city of one hundred elephants, twenty thousand horses, and more cattle than anyone can count—the city of the King of Twenty Kings? How are the kings? It is hard for me to hear down here below the ground!"

"The jungle is above our heads," said Mowgli. "I know Hathi and his sons and the other elephants, but Bagheera has killed all the horses in the village, and—what is a king?"

"I told you," said Kaa softly to the cobra— "I told you four moons ago that the city was gone."

"This city will never be gone!" the white cobra shouted. "They built it before my grandfather, and it shall be here for my sons when they grow old like me! Now, who are you?" he said to the boy in front of him.

"They call me Mowgli," was his answer. "I am from the jungle. The wolves are my people, and Kaa is my brother. But who are you?"

"I am the Keeper of the King's Treasure. I will

harm anyone who comes to steal it," the cobra hissed.

"Are there really riches here?" Mowgli asked, wondering how true the snake's story was.

"Five times since I came here, there has been treasure added. The large stone is pushed away and the treasure of a hundred kings is hidden here. But it has been a long, long time since the stone was last moved, and I think that my city has forgotten the treasures."

Mowgli looked at the cobra with sadness. "There is no city! Look up! The roots of the giant trees are tearing the stones apart!"

"Trees and men do not grow together," Kaa said firmly.

"Men have come here before," the white cobra answered. "I found them reaching around here in the dark. See for yourself what treasures I keep."

The white cobra slid forward into another room, and Kaa and Mowgli followed.

Mowgli stared with squinted eyes at the floor, then lifted up handfuls of something that glittered.

"Oh" he said, "this is like the stuff that the Man Pack play with, only this is yellow and theirs is brown."

He let the gold pieces fall and moved forward. The floor was buried under five or six feet of silver and gold coins. There were golden candlesticks, statues of men with pearls and gems at their edges, and swords, daggers, and knives with diamonds all around. There was every type of jewelry men could wear: bracelets, rings, headbands, nose rings, and necklaces, all made out of the finest gold and gems. Golden bowls and ladles lay beside jade cups. Combs and pots for perfume covered with gold powder and shimmering with sapphires, rubies, and emeralds shone in the corner.

The white cobra was right. Some men would pay anything to have this treasure. Mowgli was sure of it. But he didn't understand what these things meant. He found the knives interesting, but they didn't fit his hand as well as his own knife so he dropped them. At last Mowgli found something that really interested him. It was a three-foot-long hook, sometimes called an ankus or an elephant prod. The top was a single round, shining ruby stone. The handle was twelve inches long, making it easy to hold on to. The top of the handle was turquoise. The rest of the handle had a picture of elephants being caught. This reminded Mowgli of Hathi and made him want the ankus for his own.

"Is that not worth dying for?" the white cobra asked Mowgli.

"I don't understand," said the boy. "The other things here are hard and cold and are not for eating. But this—I want to take this with me to see it sparkle in the sun. If these treasures are all yours, will you trade this one to me for frogs, which I will bring you to eat?"

The white cobra shook with delight. "Surely, I will give it to you—until you go away."

"But I am going now. This place is dark and cold, and I want to take this stick back to the jungle."

"Do you want to know what happened to the other men who tried to take treasures from here?" asked the snake.

"No," said Mowgli. "I only want to take this stick and go home."

"But I have never allowed a man to leave here with his life! I am the Keeper of the King's

Treasures! I can't let you go," the white cobra said, and began to move toward Mowgli.

Just then, Kaa gave the ankus a kick. The sharp knife flew into the air and came down, pinning the white snake's hood to the floor. In a flash, Kaa was on top of the wiggling creature, keeping it still from head to toe. The red eyes burned and the head turned with panic from left to right.

"Kill!" said Kaa as Mowgli's hand went to his knife.

"No," he said. "I will never kill again unless it is for food. But that isn't necessary."

Mowgli forced the mouth of the white cobra open with the blade of his knife. He showed Kaa the terrible poison fangs of the snake, black in the back of his mouth.

"There is no poison left in this snake!" he said, setting the creature free. "He is too old!"

The white cobra looked at his two visitors. "I am shamed," he said. "Kill me!"

"There is too much talk of killing," said Mowgli. "We shall just go."

"Leave the king's ankus!" the white snake shouted in his loudest voice. "It will only bring evil and death."

Mowgli gave the ankus a little flip in his hand, caught it, and left without looking back at the creature. Death was not something he feared.

Both the boy and python were glad to get to the light of day once more. When they were back in their own jungle, Mowgli made the ankus glitter in the sunlight. He was almost as pleased as if he had found a bunch of new flowers to stick in his hair.

"This is brighter than Bagheera's eyes," he said with delight. "I must show it to him."

Mowgli danced off and found Bagheera drinking after a filling meal. He told the panther of his adventures and showed him the ankus. The one red stone on the dagger was enough to catch the panther's eye.

"What is this shimmering knife for?" Mowgli asked his friend.

"It was made by men to kill elephants," Bagheera said.

"But why?" Mowgli asked.

"To teach them Man's Law," the panther replied.

Mowgli shook his head, not able to understand these laws made up by men. He gave the ankus a throw and watched the sparkling knife glide through the air. It buried itself in the ground about thirty yards away. He was strangely glad to be rid of the toy. It didn't matter how pretty it was; he didn't need something that meant "death" to his friends going with him. And so he and Bagheera left, leaving the glittering knife behind in the dirt.

CHAPTER 7

Red Dog

⌒

Mowgli had many adventures, but we must tell one story at a time. This is a tale about one of the most pleasant times in his life. The jungle was his friend, but there were still a few animals out there who were a little afraid of him.

Father and Mother Wolf had grown old with time and, like all living things, finally died. Mowgli gently placed them in the cave and rolled a huge rock against the opening. He sang a sad song for them. His friends, Bagheera and Baloo, were growing old as well. Akela's age no longer allowed him to kill for himself, so Mowgli killed his friend's supper and made sure that he got enough to eat.

The younger wolves grew greater in number. When there were about forty of them, Akela told them they should form their own group and follow the Law. They should also choose a leader.

It just so happened that the wolf who fought his way to the leadership of the Pack was named Phao. Those were days of good hunting and good sleeping. No one bothered Phao's wolves, and the Pack grew fat and strong.

There were many cubs to bring to the Looking-over. Mowgli always attended this ceremony, remembering the night so many years ago when a black panther had brought a little baby into the Pack.

One evening when Mowgli was trotting across the grass to give Akela his dinner, he heard a strange and scary cry. The last time he remembered hearing this cry was when the tiger Shere Khan had hunted. The jackal would scream, letting the whole jungle know a killing had taken place.

"But no striped tigers dare kill here now," said Mowgli.

The man cub ran to the Council Rock, passing others on his way. Phao and Akela were on the Rock together when he got there. Mothers and cubs hurried off to their dens, for when they heard that cry, they knew it was no time to be out in the jungle.

Finally all grew quiet. Nothing could be heard except the breeze among the treetops. Then a wolf called from across the river. It was no wolf from the Pack. They were all at the Council Rock or in their dens. The song it sang was a long "Dhole!"

Mowgli and the others heard feet upon the rocks. A thin wolf with a touch of red in his fur, a limp right paw, and a foaming mouth flung himself into the circle. He lay gasping for air at Mowgli's feet.

"They are coming!" the wolf said. "The dhole — the Red Dog — the killers!"

"How many?" said Mowgli quickly. The Pack growled deep in their throats.

"I don't know," the thin wolf said. "But they are moving quickly. They are driving straight for the jungle and harming everything in their way."

Mowgli knew this to be true. Although the Red Dog were not as big or as smart as the wolves, they were very strong and traveled in large packs. Usually no less than a hundred traveled together. A wolf pack was large at forty.

Mowgli hated the Red Dog. They did not smell like jungle animals, they did not live in caves, and above all, they had hair between their toes. Wolves were clean-footed. Hathi had always said how terrible a Red Dog pack could be. Even he moved aside when they came to the jungle.

Akela knew things about the dholes, too. "Go north and lie down," he told Mowgli. "Wait for them to leave."

"How can I catch little fish or sleep under a tree while the Pack is fighting?" Mowgli asked.

"You don't know the Red Dog," said Akela. "They fight to the death."

"Then I shall do what I can! We will need every wolf! You and Phao must get the battle ready. I will go to count the dogs!"

"But that will mean death for you!" Akela reminded him once more.

"Don't be so sure!" Mowgli shouted with excitement as he hurried off into the darkness, hardly looking where he was going. Because he was not paying attention, he tripped on something and fell full onto the ground.

"Pssssss!" said Kaa angrily.

"I'm sorry, Kaa," said Mowgli, picking himself up. "I was looking for you. Each time I see you,

you are longer and thicker! There is no other like you in the jungle. You are wise and old and strong, most beautiful Kaa."

"You must need my help," the snake hissed.

The boy reached out in the darkness and snuggled in comfortably against the snake. Then he told him all that had happened in the jungle that night.

"How many are there?" the snake asked.

"I have not yet seen. I was hoping you could help me. But oh, Kaa." Mowgli stopped to wiggle with joy. "It will be such good hunting!"

"You must not hunt!" the worried snake cried. "Remember, you are a man! Let the wolves fight the dogs!"

"It is true that I am a man, but my heart says I am also a wolf. I will be a wolf until the dholes have gone by."

The snake answered, "What will your heart say when the dhole pack reaches us?"

"They must swim the Waingunga River. I thought I would greet them with my knife. I could hurt them, and then send them on down the river to the Wolf Pack," Mowgli said proudly.

"There are too many for that to work," Kaa answered.

"What do you think I should do?" the man cub asked with disappointment.

"Climb on," said the python. "We will go to the river and I will show you what is to be done against the dholes."

As he turned for the stream, Mowgli tucked his left arm around Kaa's neck, dropped his right arm close to his body, and straightened his feet. The swim through the water was swift. Mowgli looked from side to side, sniffing quickly as they went along. Finally Kaa stopped by twisting his long tail around a sunken rock. He held Mowgli tightly while the water raced on.

"This is called the Place of Death," said the boy. "It is dangerous here with the fast water and the jagged rocks. And there is no bank to climb out on. Why do we come here?"

Two steep walls rose on either side of the pair.

"Look at this," said the snake, pointing to a pile of rocks and bones. Among the bones lay the skeletons of a young deer and buffalo.

"They fell from above?" Mowgli asked.

"Yes," Kaa answered. "A fall from above here could kill an animal in a few ways. The fall alone could kill it, or the river could carry it away. There is no way out."

Mowgli stared at the walls, taking in especially how high they were.

"If a pack of dogs were to follow a man cub above, and the man cub happened to fall over a cliff into this water below (safely into the curves of a python), and the pack happened to fall into this cave after him (with no one to catch them), I think that many dogs would meet their death," the snake said.

"I have jumped twice as far for fun," Mowgli said quietly. "But I am not a dhole. Have you been to the land above?"

"Don't worry, Little Brother," Kaa said. "I have been there before. This plan will work. I will be here to safely catch you as you lead the rest of the pack over the cliff."

Mowgli, excited by the plan, swam downstream. He paddled toward the faraway bank where he could get out of the water and meet the trail that led to the land above.

Kaa swam downstream as well, but found his way to Phao and Akela, who were listening to the night noises.

"Where are the dogs?" asked Phao.

"And where is my man cub?" asked Akela.

"Wait here for the dhole tomorrow. Be glad that the man cub and I will be seeing them first."

Kaa flashed upstream again and found himself in the middle of the ravine looking upward at the cliff. He saw Mowgli's head move against the black background of the stars. Then there was a whizz in the air, the sound of a body falling, and the next minute the boy was at rest again in the loop of Kaa's body.

Kaa smiled. Tomorrow they would do the same, only dozens of dogs would follow the jump off the cliff—not knowing the ground in front of them had disappeared.

⌒

The next day, just after noon, Mowgli settled himself in a tree along the path where the thin wolf had said the dogs would come. He sat very still and sharpened his knife, singing softly to himself. It wasn't long before he heard the patter of feet and smelled the awful smell of the dhole pack as they came trotting across the jungle path. Mowgli watched the sharp pointy head of the lead dog sniffing along the trail.

"Good hunting!" Mowgli said from a branch in the tree that stuck out far above the ground.

The lead dog looked up and the others stopped behind him. There were dozens and dozens of red dogs with low-hung tails, heavy shoulders, and hungry mouths. There must have been two hundred in the group below Mowgli.

"Why are you here?" asked Mowgli.

"The jungle belongs to no one!" said the leader. "We are welcome here as much as you."

Mowgli knew he must anger the dogs if they were to chase him. "Go back to where you came from and eat lizards!" the man cub yelled.

"Come down from that tree, you tree-ape!" yelled the pack. This was exactly the reaction Mowgli wanted. He teased the dogs until they could take it no more.

Mowgli moved like a monkey into the next tree, then to the next, then to the next. The pack followed him, their heads lifted high watching the man cub leap through the air. Every now and then Mowgli would pretend to fall, and the pack would tumble over one another in their hurry to get the boy.

When Mowgli got near the cliff, he slipped down a tree trunk and ran like the wind for the edge, where the dogs would follow him over. It was a long run—two miles in all—and Mowgli needed to keep the dogs running at full speed behind him. As the cliff drew near, Mowgli prepared himself for his jump. When it finally appeared, the man cub leapt out with all his strength. He felt himself fall swiftly down, with the hot breath of the dogs still behind him. The next thing he knew, he was tucked safely in Kaa's coiled body. Overhead, he could hear the short yells of the Red Dog as they fell, one after another, over the cliff and into the rocks and water below. The water raged on, and the dogs fought their way downstream. Their cries of anger echoed in the cave.

Their true terror came, however, when they came upon the Wolf Pack waiting for them half a mile downstream. Burning eyes and low growls lined the bank. The entire Pack flung themselves at the dogs as they came sailing down the rapid water. The long fight, which had begun with Mowgli in a tree, ended with Mowgli fighting as a member of the Wolf Pack. Akela, weak from his last fight, lay beside the boy.

"This is the end for me, Little Brother," he said. "I knew I would die near you."

Mowgli took the wolf's head and placed it on his knees, then put his arms around Akela's neck.

"It's been a long time since I saw that little man cub in the dust," Akela said.

"No, Akela, I am a wolf. I am one of the Pack! I have no wish to be a man!" Mowgli said firmly.

"Yet you are a man, Little Brother. I owe you my life, and today you have saved the Pack once again. I saved you when you were a baby, but you have saved me as well. We are even. Go to your people. The hunting is over. Go to your people."

"I will never go!" Mowgli said in anger. "I will hunt alone in the jungle."

"After the summer comes the rains, and after the rains comes the spring. Go back before you are forced to go back," said Akela.

"Who will force me?" Mowgli asked.

"You will force yourself," said Akela. "Go back to your people. Go back to Man."

"When I am forced to go, I will," said Mowgli.

"There is nothing more to say," said Akela. "Little Brother, can you help me to stand?"

Very carefully and gently, Mowgli lifted Akela to his feet. The Lone Wolf drew a deep breath and began to howl the Death Song that a leader of the Pack should sing when he dies. It grew louder and louder as he went on, ringing far across the river until it came to the end. Akela shook himself away from Mowgli for an instant, leapt into the air, and fell backward onto the cold hard ground.

"Howl, dogs! Howl! A wolf has died tonight!" said Phao when he saw Mowgli holding Akela. "A very special wolf has died tonight."

CHAPTER 8

The Spring Running

Two years after the death of Akela, Mowgli turned seventeen years old. To look at him, though, he appeared much older. His hard exercise, good eating habits, and daily baths gave him strength and a body that made him look more like a man than a boy. He could swing by one hand from the top branch of a tree for half an hour at a time. He could stop a young buck in the middle of its gallop and throw it sideways by its head. He could even catch and toss the big blue wild boars that lived in the Marshes of the North.

The jungle animals all feared him. When he walked the paths, everyone cleared out of his way. And yet the look in his eyes was always gentle. Even when he fought, his eyes never blazed as Bagheera's did. They only grew more and more interested and excited.

One day, Mowgli and Bagheera were lying upon the side of a hill overlooking the Waingunga River. Somewhere, down in the woods below, a bird was trying to sing the first few notes of his spring song. It was short, and not quite right, but Bagheera heard it.

"The Time of New Talk is near," growled the panther, flipping his tail.

"I hear," Mowgli answered.

"That is the scarlet woodpecker," said Bagheera. "He has not forgotten. Now I, too, must remember my song." The panther began purring and humming to himself, stopping over and over, disappointed in how he sounded.

"I don't see any game here," said Mowgli.

"Little Brother, that is not my killing song. That is my spring song."

"I had forgotten. I will know when the Time of New Talk is here because you and the others will run away and leave me alone." Mowgli spoke with anger in his voice.

"We don't always——"

"Yes, you do," said Mowgli, pointing his finger angrily. "You do run away and I, the Master of the Jungle, must walk alone. Some members of the jungle will not even listen to me."

"At the Time of New Talk," said the panther, "perhaps they don't hear?"

Mowgli lay back with his head on his arms. "I do not know——nor do I care," he said sleepily. "Let us sleep, Bagheera. Make me a rest for my head."

The panther lay down again with a sigh, listening to the woodpecker in the distance.

In an Indian jungle, the seasons slide one into

the other, almost without notice. There seem to be only two seasons—wet and dry. But if you look closely, you will find that there are four. Spring is the most wonderful, because it works to make the earth feel new and young again.

There is one day when all things are tired, and the very smells as they drift through the air are old and used. It is hard to explain. It is easier to just feel it. There is another day, which looks exactly the same as the first, when all the smells are new and delightful. A little rain falls and all the trees and the bushes and the bamboos and the mosses and the juicy-leaved plants wake with a noise of growing that you can almost hear. And under this noise runs, day and night, a deep hum. That is the noise of the spring—a boom that isn't bees, nor falling water, nor the wind in treetops, but the purring of the warm, happy world.

Mowgli had always delighted in the turn of the seasons. But this spring was different. He had been looking forward to the morning when the smells should change ever since the bamboo shoots had turned spotty brown. But when the morning came, and Mor the peacock, shining in bronze and blue and gold, cried it aloud all along the woods, Mowgli opened his mouth to send on the cry, and the words choked between his teeth. A feeling came over him that began at his toes and ended in his hair — a feeling of pure unhappiness.

"The smells have changed!" screamed Mor after waiting for Mowgli's answer. "Where is your call?"

Mowgli never replied. A light spring rain began, causing the jungle folk to talk at once. Mowgli only spoke softly to himself.

"I have eaten good food," he said. "I have drunk good water. But my stomach is heavy and I have talked very badly to Bagheera and the others. I am hot and then I am cold, and then I am neither hot nor cold. I am angry at what I cannot see. It is time for me to go! Tonight I will leave! I will make a spring run to the Marshes of the North and back again. No one will even know. For when the spring comes, each animal is too busy with himself to care about others. Let the Red Dog come or let someone need food and they call for Mowgli. But when the magic of spring comes, the jungle goes mad. They forget I am the Master of the Jungle."

Mowgli killed his supper early that evening and ate little so he would be in good shape for the spring run. He ate alone because all the jungle animals were away singing or fighting. Forgetting his unhappiness, Mowgli sang aloud with pure delight as he set off on his run.

He ran a long way, sometimes shouting, sometimes singing to himself. He was the happiest thing in all the jungle that night until the smell of the flowers warned him that he was near the marshes. When he finally got there, he went out to the middle of the swamp, bothering only the ducks as he ran, and sat down on a moss-coated tree trunk in the black water. No one took any notice of Mowgli sitting among the flowers, humming songs without words. All his unhappiness seemed to have been left behind in his own jungle. He was just about to begin a loud burst of song when it came back again—ten times worse than before.

This time Mowgli was frightened. "It is here also!" he said aloud. "It has followed me!" The night noises grew louder, and his sadness grew as well. Mowgli looked around, hoping to see what it was that was making him feel so unhappy. He howled, hoping one of his brothers would hear and come see him. But no one came, and his heart felt only heavier until . . .

"I must have eaten poison!" he said at once. "That's it! It must be that in some careless way I ate poison and my bravery and strength are dying. Mowgli has never been afraid before. And yet here I am, frightened. That is a true sign I have eaten poison.

"And look, no one even cares. They sing and howl and fight and run in the moonlight and here I am dying in the marshes from the poison I have eaten." Mowgli felt so sorry for himself that he nearly cried.

"They will not find me lying here in this black water. No, I will go back to my own jungle and I will die upon the Council Rock and Bagheera, whom I love, may comfort me in the end."

A large warm tear splashed down on his knee. But as upset as he was, he wanted to continue his spring run. He had barely started when he came upon the village at the foot of the marsh.

It had been a long time since Mowgli had had anything to do with Man. But tonight he felt drawn to them.

"I will look," he said, "as I did in the old days, and I will see how the Man Pack has changed."

Forgetting that he was no longer in his own jungle, where he could do what he pleased, he stomped carelessly through the grasses until he came to the hut where the light stood. Three or four dogs barked at him.

"Ho!" said Mowgli, silencing the dogs. He waited only seconds before the hut door opened. A woman peeked out into the darkness. A child cried, and the woman said over her shoulder, "Sleep, it was only a jackal waking the dogs. Morning will be here soon."

Mowgli began to shake. He knew the voice well and he cried out, waiting for an answer.

"Messua! Oh, Messua!"

"Who calls?" said the woman, a quiver in her own voice.

"Have you forgotten me?" said Mowgli.

"If it is you," she said, "what name did I give you?" She had half shut the door, and her hand was holding her chest.

"Nathoo! Oh, Nathoo!" said Mowgli.

"Come, my son," she called, and Mowgli stepped into the light and looked full at Messua. She was older, and her hair was gray, but her eyes and her voice had not changed. Her eyes traveled up and down the older boy standing before her, for she had last seen him as a youngster.

"My son," she stammered. "But you are no longer my son. You are a God of the Woods!"

Mowgli stood in the red light of the oil lamp, strong, tall, and handsome. His long black hair swept over his shoulders, and his knife swung at his neck. His head was crowned with a wreath of white jasmine flowers, and he could easily have been mistaken for some wild god of a jungle legend. A little boy, half asleep on a cot, sprang up and screamed aloud with fright. Messua turned to calm him while Mowgli looked around the room, remembering the human belongings he had last seen so long ago.

"Will you eat and drink with us?" Messua asked. "Everything I have is yours. We owe our lives to you. But are you Nathoo, or a God of the Jungle?"

"I am Nathoo," said Mowgli. "I am very far from my own place. I saw this light and came here. I didn't know I would find you."

The woman smiled. "We own a little land here. It is not so nice as at the old village, but we do not need much. There are just the two of us."

"Where is your husband?" asked Mowgli.

"He is dead a year now," she answered.

"And he?" Mowgli asked, pointing to the child.

"My son that was born two rains ago. If you are a God of the Jungle, give him a spell so he may be safe."

She lifted up the child who, forgetting to be frightened, reached out to play with the knife that hung on Mowgli's chest. Mowgli moved the little fingers aside very carefully.

"And if you are Nathoo," Messua went on, beginning to cry now, "then he is your younger brother. Give him an older brother's blessing."

Mowgli answered. "What do I know about blessings? I am neither a God of the Jungle nor a brother to this boy. Oh, Mother, my heart is so heavy." He shivered.

"I will make a fire and you shall drink warm milk," his mother said.

Mowgli sat down, muttering with his face in his hands. A strange feeling he had never felt before was running through him. He felt dizzy and a little sick. He drank the warm milk in gulps. Messua patted him on the shoulder now and then, still not quite sure if he was her son Nathoo of long ago or some wonderful jungle being. But she was glad to feel that he was flesh and blood.

"Son," she asked, her eyes full of pride, "has anyone ever told you how handsome you are?"

"Hah?" said Mowgli, for naturally he had never heard anything of the kind.

Messua laughed softly and happily. The look in his face was enough for her.

"I am the first one to tell you, then?" she asked. "It is only right that a mother should be the first to say these things. You are so very hand-some. Never have I looked upon such a man."

Mowgli twisted his head and tried to see over his shoulder. Messua laughed again for so long that finally Mowgli laughed with her. Even the child joined in, running between Mowgli and his mother.

The warm milk soon took effect and Mowgli curled up. Within a minute he was in a deep sleep. Messua moved the hair back from his eyes, threw a cloth over him, and was happy.

Mowgli slept the rest of the night, and all of the next day. Everything he knew from living in the jungle told him that he was safe and that there was nothing to fear. He woke at last with a leap that shook the hut, for the cloth covering his face made him dream of traps. He stood with his hand on his knife, ready for a fight.

Messua laughed and put the evening meal in front of him. There were only a few little cakes baked over the smoky fire, some rice, and some fruit—just enough to get him by until his evening kill.

It didn't take long for Mowgli to get hungry and restless. He wanted to finish his spring running, but the child insisted on sitting in his arms. And Messua said his hair must be combed out before he left.

She sang as she combed his hair and spoke softly of her younger days in the jungle. She now called Mowgli her son. When it was time for him to leave, she threw her arms around his neck again and again.

"Come back!" she whispered. "Son or no son,

come back, for I love thee. By night or by day, this door is never shut to you."

The child was crying because the man with the shiny knife was going away.

Mowgli's throat felt as though the cords in it were being pulled, and his voice seemed to be dragged from it as he answered. "I will surely come back."

He met Gray Brother as he left and looked at him with disappointment. "I have a little cry against you, Gray Brother. Why didn't you come when I needed you in the marsh? I called for my brothers! I called for you!"

"We were singing new songs in the jungle, for this is the Time of New Talk. Remember?" said Gray Brother.

"Yes, yes," muttered Mowgli.

"As soon as the songs were sung, I followed your trail. I ran from all the others and followed you. But what are you doing with the Man Pack?"

"If you had come when I called, this never would have happened," Mowgli said, running faster.

"But I am here now," Gray Brother said.

"But will you always follow me?" asked Mowgli.

They were running as they talked. Gray Brother trotted on a bit before answering. "Man cub, Master of the Jungle, sometimes I forget a little bit in the spring, but I follow you always."

"You know how I feel, Gray Brother. You know the truth! Run on ahead to the Council Rock and cry to all. I will talk when they are gathered."

Gray Brother ran ahead, crying, "The Master of the Jungle goes back to Man! Come to the Council Rock." And the happy listeners only answered, "He will come back in the summer heat. The rains will bring him back. Run and sing with us, Gray Brother. Forget about Mowgli and the Council Rock!"

"But the Master of the Jungle is going back to Man!" Gray Brother repeated.

So when Mowgli, with a heavy heart, came up through the rocks to the place where he was to speak, he found only Baloo, who was nearly blind in his old age, and the cold-blooded Kaa coiled around Akela's empty seat.

"So this is the end?" said Kaa as Mowgli threw himself down on the rock, his face in his hands.

"My strength is gone from me, and it is not any poison. I hear someone following me, but when I turn around, there is no one there. I call and no one answers. I lie down but I do not rest. I run the spring running, but I am not made still. I bathe, but I am not cooled. I hate to kill, but I have not the heart to fight if not to kill. I do not know what to do."

Kaa answered his friend. "Mowgli, you will go to Man in the end, even though the jungle does not throw you out."

The friends looked at one another and then at Mowgli.

"The jungle does not want me out?" Mowgli answered, not believing what he was hearing.

Gray Brother and his friends growled, saying, "So long as we live, no one shall dare—" But Baloo stopped them.

"Mowgli, I taught you the Law. I cannot see the rocks well before me, but I can see far. Little frog, take your own path. Make your own life with the Man Pack. But when there is need of foot or tooth or eye, or a word passed on at night, remember, Master of the Jungle, the jungle is yours to call."

"My brothers," cried Mowgli throwing up his arms with a sob. "I don't know what to do! I would not go, but I feel like I am being pulled. How can I leave?"

"Listen, dearest of all to me," said Baloo. "There is nothing here to hold you back. I remember that great day many years ago when you were that little boy playing in the pebbles at this Council Rock. Bagheera bought you for the price of a newly killed bull. There are only two of us left from that looking-over. The old Wolf Pack is long since dead. Shere Khan is gone. Akela died among the dholes. Nothing remains but old bones. You are not asking to leave the Pack. You are the Master of the Jungle changing your trail."

"But Bagheera and the bull that bought me," said Mowgli. "I would not—"

Suddenly there was a roar and crash in the bushes below, and Bagheera, light, strong, and terrible as always, stood before him.

"It was a long hunt, but a bull lies dead in the bushes, Little Brother," Bagheera said. "We are even now. We owe each other nothing." He licked Mowgli's foot. "Remember, Bagheera loved you," the panther cried, then ran swiftly away. At the bottom of the hill, he cried again, long and loud,

"Good hunting on the new trails, Master of the Jungle! Remember, Bagheera loved you!"

"You have heard it all," said Baloo. "There is no more. Go now. But first come to me, little frog. Come to me."

"It is hard to make such choices," said Kaa as Mowgli sobbed and sobbed. The young man's head was resting on the snake, and his arms were wrapped around the neck of the creature while Baloo tried hard to lick his feet. Mowgli felt the warmth of his friends spread through him.

"The stars are thin," said Gray Brother, raising his nose to the dawn wind. "Where shall we go today, my friends? For from now on, just as our Master, we, too, will follow new trails."

And so, with a final good-bye, Mowgli's stories in the jungle came to an end.

What Do *You* Think?
Questions for Discussion

ᘓ

Have you ever been around a toddler who keeps asking the question "Why?" Does your teacher call on you in class with questions from your homework? Do your parents ask you questions about your day at the dinner table? We are always surrounded by questions that need a specific response. But is it possible to have a question with no right answer?

The following questions are about the book you just read. But this is not a quiz! They are designed to help you look at the people, places, and events in the story from different angles. These questions do not have specific answers. Instead, they might make you think of the story in a completely new way.

Think carefully about each question and enjoy discovering more about this classic story.

1. Tabaqi the jackal is known for making trouble and telling lies. Do you know anyone like this? Have you ever told a lie?

2. Why do you suppose it is so important for the animals to follow the Law of the Jungle? What kind of rules do you live by?

3. When Bagheera warns Mowgli to be careful around Shere Khan, the boy laughs and says he is not afraid so long as he has Baloo, Bagheera, and the Pack. Why do you suppose he feels this way? How would you have reacted in his place?

4. Mowgli is raised by wolves and taught by a bear. How does this make him different from the

villagers? If you could live with any kind of animal, what would it be?

5. Kaa says that he is angry at the monkeys for calling him names. Has anyone ever made fun of you? How did it make you feel?

6. As far as the villagers are concerned, the only good thing about Mowgli is his strength. What do you think some of his other good qualities are? What is your best quality?

7. How do the villagers react when they see Bagheera in Messua's hut? What would you have done in their place? What is the scariest thing that has ever happened to you?

8. Why does Mowgli want the King's ankus? How do you suppose he feels when the white cobra says that he cannot have it? Have you ever wanted something you were told you couldn't have?

9. Do you think Mowgli's plan to stop the Red Dog is brave or foolish? Would you have gone

through with it? What is the bravest thing you've ever done?

10. Kaa tells Mowgli that it is hard to make choices. What kind of choices must Mowgli make? Have you ever had to make a hard decision?

Afterword

by Arthur Pober, Ed.D.

ᘉ

First impressions are important.

Whether we are meeting new people, going to new places, or picking up a book unknown to us, first impressions count for a lot. They can lead to warm, lasting memories or can make us shy away from any future encounters.

Can you recall your own first impressions and earliest memories of reading the classics?

Do you remember wading through pages and pages of text to prepare for an exam? Or were you the child who hid under the blanket to read with a flashlight, joining forces with Robin Hood to save Maid Marian? Do you remember only how long it took you to read a lengthy novel such as *Little Women*? Or did you become best friends with the March sisters?

Even for a gifted young reader, getting through long chapters with dense language can easily become overwhelming and can obscure the richness of the story and its characters. Reading an abridged, newly crafted version of a classic novel can be the gentle introduction a child needs to explore the characters and storyline without the frustration of difficult vocabulary and complex themes.

Reading an abridged version of a classic novel gives the young reader a sense of independence and the satisfaction of finishing a "grown-up" book. And when a child is engaged with and inspired by a classic story, the tone is set for further exploration of the story's themes, characters, history, and details. As a child's reading skills advance, the desire to tackle the original, unabridged version of the story will naturally emerge.

If made accessible to young readers, these stories can become invaluable tools for understanding themselves in the context of their families and social environments. This is why the Classic Starts series includes questions that stimulate discussion regarding the impact and social relevance of the characters and stories today. These questions can foster lively conversations between children and their parents or teachers. When we look at the issues, values, and standards of past times in terms of how we live now, we can appreciate literature's classic tales in a very personal and engaging way.

Share your love of reading the classics with a young child, and introduce an imaginary world real enough to last a lifetime.

Dr. Arthur Pober, Ed.D.

Dr. Arthur Pober has spent more than twenty years in the fields of early childhood and gifted education. He is the former principal of one of the world's oldest laboratory schools for gifted youngsters, Hunter College Elementary School, and former Director of Magnet Schools for the Gifted and Talented for more than 25,000 youngsters in New York City.

Dr. Pober is a recognized authority in the areas of media and child protection and is currently the U.S. representative to the European Institute for the Media and European Advertising Standards Alliance.

Explore these wonderful stories in our
Classic Starts™ library.

Great Expectations
Greek Myths
Grimm's Fairy Tales
Gulliver's Travels
Heidi
The Hunchback of Notre-Dame
Journey to the Center of the Earth
The Jungle Book
The Last of the Mohicans
Little Lord Fauntleroy
Little Men
A Little Princess
Little Women
The Man in the Iron Mask
Moby-Dick
The Odyssey
Oliver Twist
Peter Pan
The Phantom of the Opera
Pinocchio